PROS AND CONS

THE DEBATE ABOUT VACCINES

by Patricia Hutchison

FOCUS READERS

FOCUS READERS

www.focusreaders.com

Focus Readers is distributed by North Star Editions:
sales@northstareditions.com | 888-417-0195

Produced for Focus Readers by Red Line Editorial.

Photographs ©: SelectStock/iStockphoto, cover, 1; loonger/iStockphoto, 4–5; Red Line Editorial, 7, 22; Steve Debenport/iStockphoto, 8–9, 44; Yanosh Nemesh/iStockphoto, 11, 28, 35; Devil007/Shutterstock Images, 13; versevend/iStockphoto, 14–15; Remains/iStockphoto, 17; Alf Ribeiro/Shutterstock Images, 19; brunoat/iStockphoto, 20–21; DETart21/iStockphoto, 24; Sean Warren/iStockphoto, 26–27; Image Source/iStockphoto, 31, 45; Antonio Scorza/Shutterstock Images, 32–33; frank60/Shutterstock Images, 36, 41; adamkaz/iStockphoto, 38–39; PureRadiancePhoto/Shutterstock Images, 42

ISBN
978-1-63517-527-1 (hardcover)
978-1-63517-599-8 (paperback)
978-1-63517-743-5 (ebook pdf)
978-1-63517-671-1 (hosted ebook)

Library of Congress Control Number: 2017948116

Printed in the United States of America
Mankato, MN
November, 2017

ABOUT THE AUTHOR

Patricia Hutchison is a former teacher. She likes to write nonfiction books about many topics. When she is not writing, Patricia enjoys traveling with her husband, children, and grandchildren.

TABLE OF CONTENTS

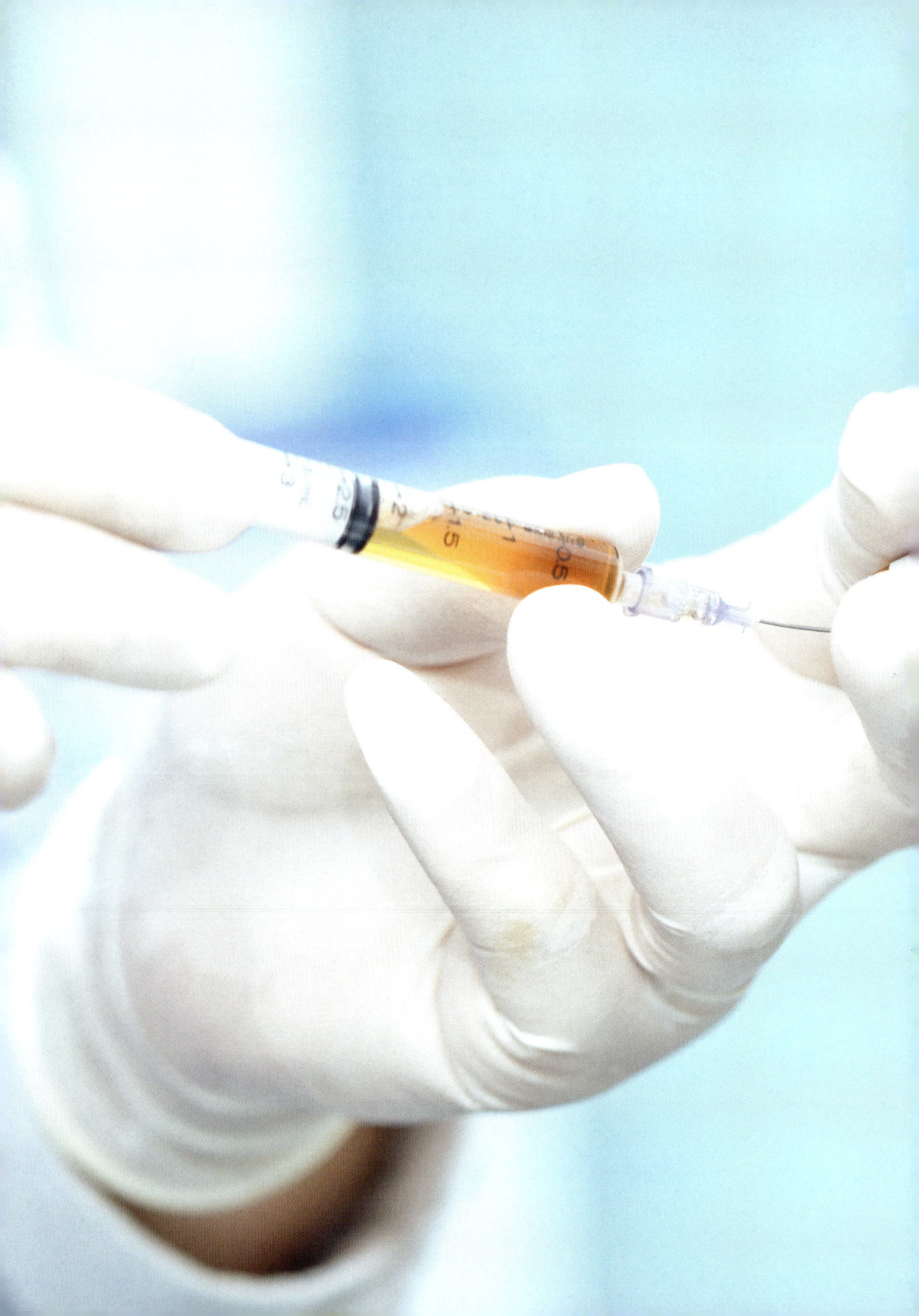

CHAPTER 1

UNDERSTANDING VACCINES

Vaccines are designed to prevent people from getting sick. When germs enter a person's body, they multiply and attack healthy cells. The body uses three kinds of white blood cells to fight back. They are macrophages, B-lymphocytes, and T-lymphocytes. Macrophages remove germs from the bloodstream. When a disease enters the body, macrophages swoop in and gobble up germs. But dangerous **antigens** are left behind.

Many vaccines are administered as shots.

Lymphocytes help fight back. The body has two kinds of these specialized blood cells. B-lymphocytes produce **antibodies**. Antibodies destroy the antigens and prevent them from attacking healthy cells. Meanwhile, T-lymphocytes invade cells that have already been infected. A few T-lymphocytes stay around even after the germs are gone. If the same kind of germ invades again, the T-lymphocytes remember it. They fight the infection before the person even feels sick. This is known as immunity.

Vaccines imitate infections. Antigens in the vaccine cause the white blood cells to respond just like they would to an infection. T-lymphocytes are left behind to fight the same germs in the future. After a few doses of a vaccine, most people are immune to the disease.

Scientists produce many kinds of vaccines. Live vaccines contain a weakened form of a virus or bacteria. The weakened germs cannot reproduce easily. They will not make a person sick. Scientists also make inactivated vaccines. The germs in these vaccines are killed with heat or chemicals. For this reason, inactivated vaccines are easier to store and handle.

HOW A VACCINE WORKS

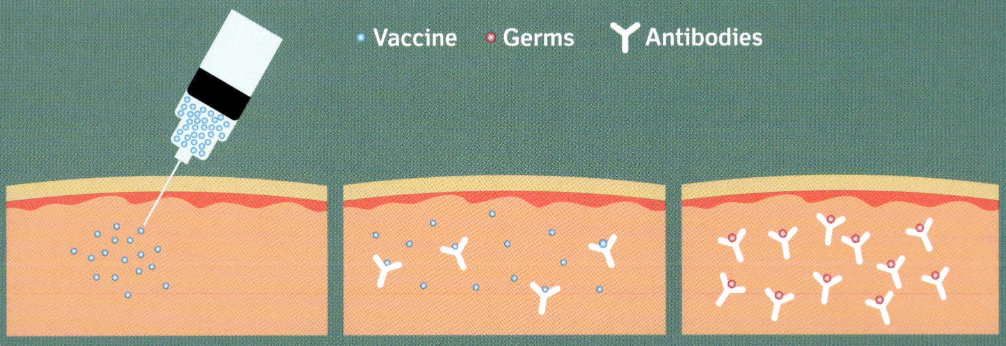

Dead or weakened germs in the vaccine enter a person's body.

The body responds to the vaccine as it would to an infection.

Antibodies remain in the body to fight the same germs in the future.

CHAPTER 2

PRO
VACCINES PREVENT DEADLY DISEASES

Vaccines prevent illnesses that are dangerous or even deadly. For instance, smallpox killed nearly 300 million people in the 1900s. But through the years, millions of people received the smallpox vaccine. Fewer people got the disease. By 1980, smallpox had disappeared. Measles, mumps, tetanus, and polio were once common diseases, too. But because of vaccines, these illnesses are rare in most countries.

Some vaccines are for serious diseases, while others are for common illnesses such as the flu.

The measles virus causes a sore throat, a fever, and a rash. It can have serious **complications**, too. These include **pneumonia** and blindness. Measles can also cause swelling of the brain or even death.

The measles vaccine was introduced in 1963. Before the vaccine, approximately four million people in the United States got measles each year. By 2004, there were only 37 cases of measles. Measles vaccines had saved more than 20 million lives worldwide by 2015.

Mumps is another viral infection. People with mumps have swollen glands under their ears. Mumps can cause the **membranes** that surround the spinal cord to swell. Some people become deaf or even die as a result.

Mumps spreads easily. More than 200,000 people got the disease in 1964. A live vaccine was created in 1967. Before this vaccine, more than

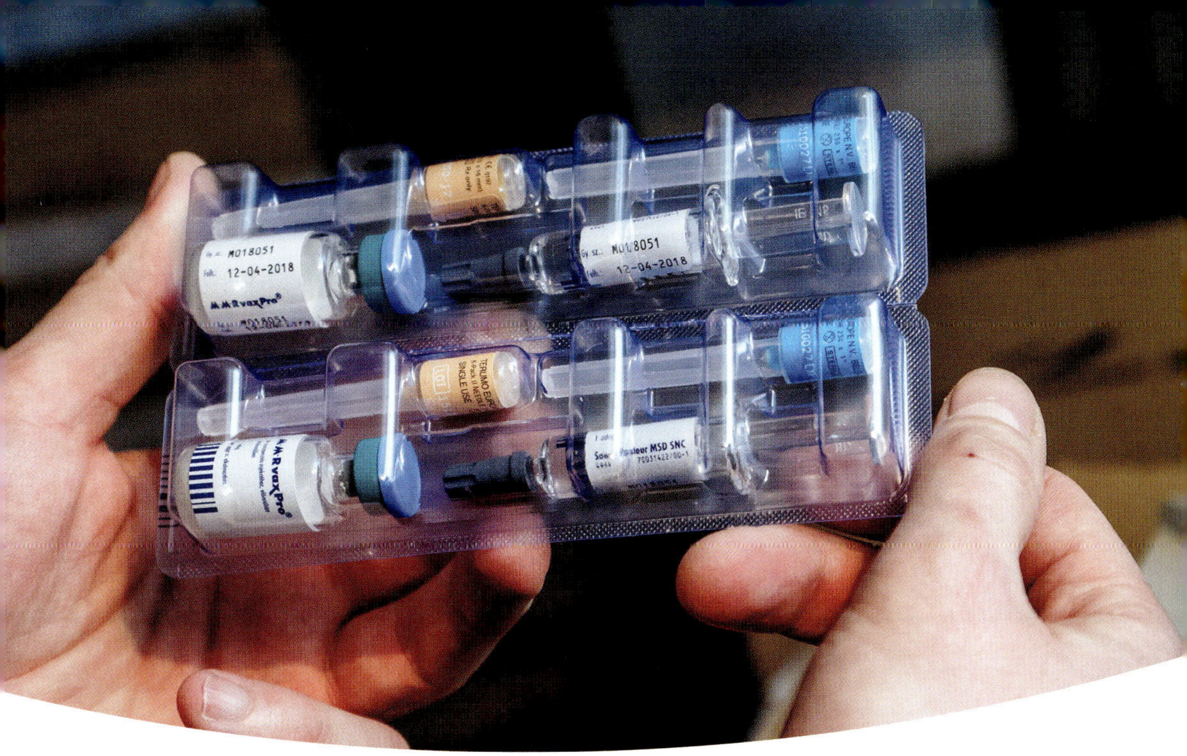

The MMR vaccine protects against measles, mumps, and rubella.

150,000 people got mumps each year. Now there are fewer than 3,000 cases of mumps most years.

Tetanus is caused by bacteria. The bacteria produce a toxin that attacks the person's **nervous system**. The person's neck and jaw muscles tighten. The spasms travel to other muscles in the body, too. Soon the person cannot move at all. Most people who get tetanus die from the disease.

In the early 1940s, approximately 500 to 600 people in the United States got tetanus each year. A tetanus vaccine was introduced in the late 1940s. The number of people who get tetanus has gone down steadily since then. Between 1995 and 2015, there were fewer than 50 cases of tetanus reported each year in the United States.

Polio can spread quickly. In many people, the virus passes out of the body without making them sick. But these people can still infect others. In some cases, the polio virus attacks a person's nervous system. Less than 1 percent of people develop a high fever. Their limbs become stiff.

DID YOU KNOW?

Vaccines against measles, mumps, tetanus, and polio save more than two million lives each year.

Tetanus bacteria often enter a person's body when a cut comes in contact with a rusty object.

Most recover completely. But some become **paralyzed**. They may have a disability for the rest of their lives.

A scientist invented a polio vaccine in 1953. Since then, millions of people around the world have received the vaccine. In 1988, polio caused 350,000 people around the world to become paralyzed. By 2016, fewer than 40 cases were reported.

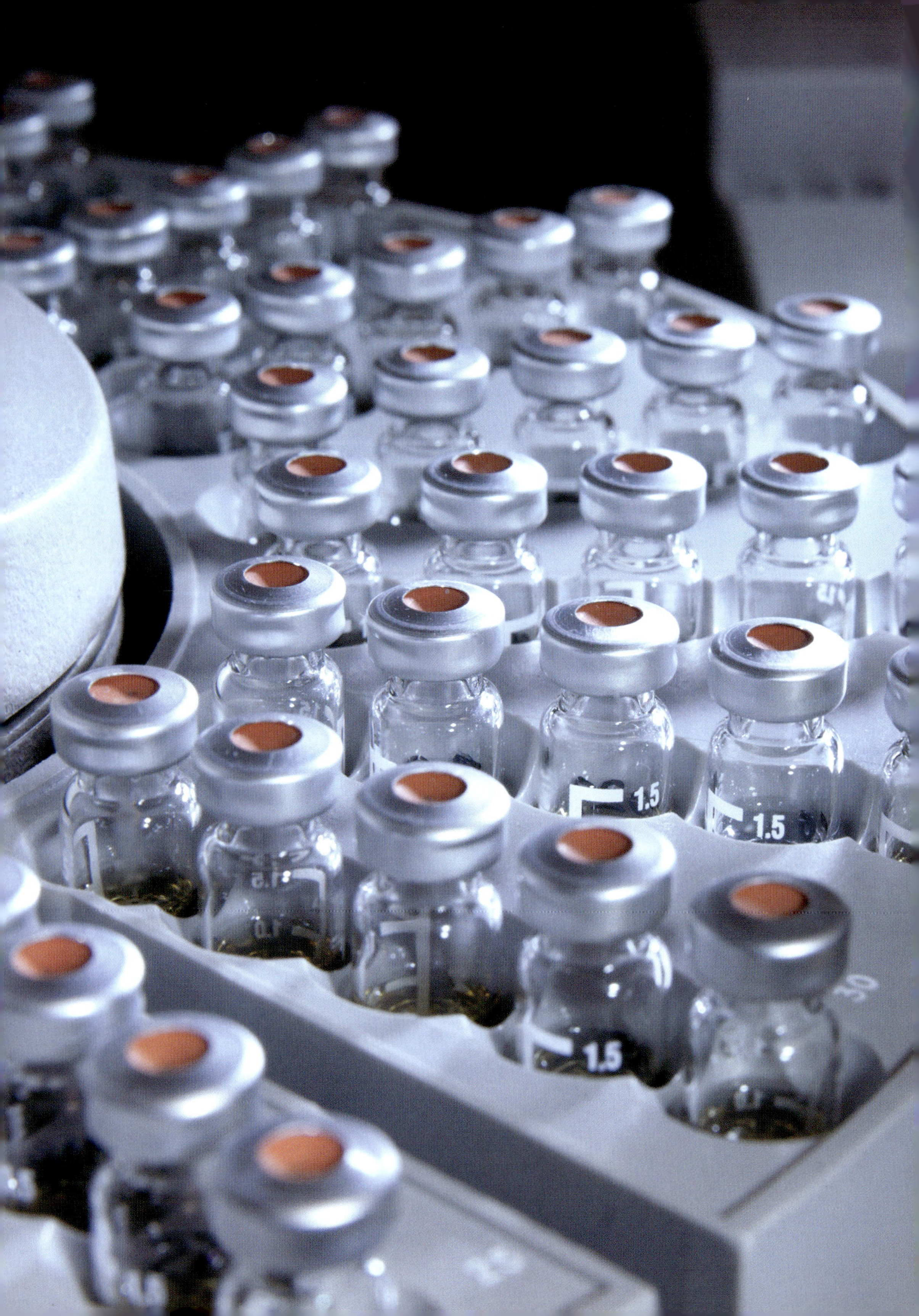
1.5
1.5
1.5
30

CHAPTER 3

PRO

VACCINES ARE SAFE AND COST-EFFECTIVE

In the United States, the Food and Drug Administration (FDA) monitors vaccines. This organization makes sure each vaccine goes through many tests before it is approved for worldwide use. First, scientists identify the antigens that could help prevent a disease. Then they test the vaccine on tissue samples and animals. They make sure it will be safe and effective.

Autosamplers help scientists study and test vaccines.

Next, a manufacturer must get permission to make and test the vaccine. The manufacturer submits an application to the FDA. The FDA must approve or deny the application within 30 days.

After the FDA approves the application, the vaccine goes through three phases of testing. First, the vaccine is given to a small group of approximately 30 people. This test helps determine if the vaccine is safe. It also shows whether the vaccine provides immunity in humans. If the vaccine passes these tests, it goes on to the second phase. In this phase, hundreds of people receive the vaccine. The company also makes decisions about doses and schedules.

If these tests are successful, the vaccine moves to the third phase. This phase uses larger **trials**. They involve thousands of people. Researchers look for serious side effects that might not

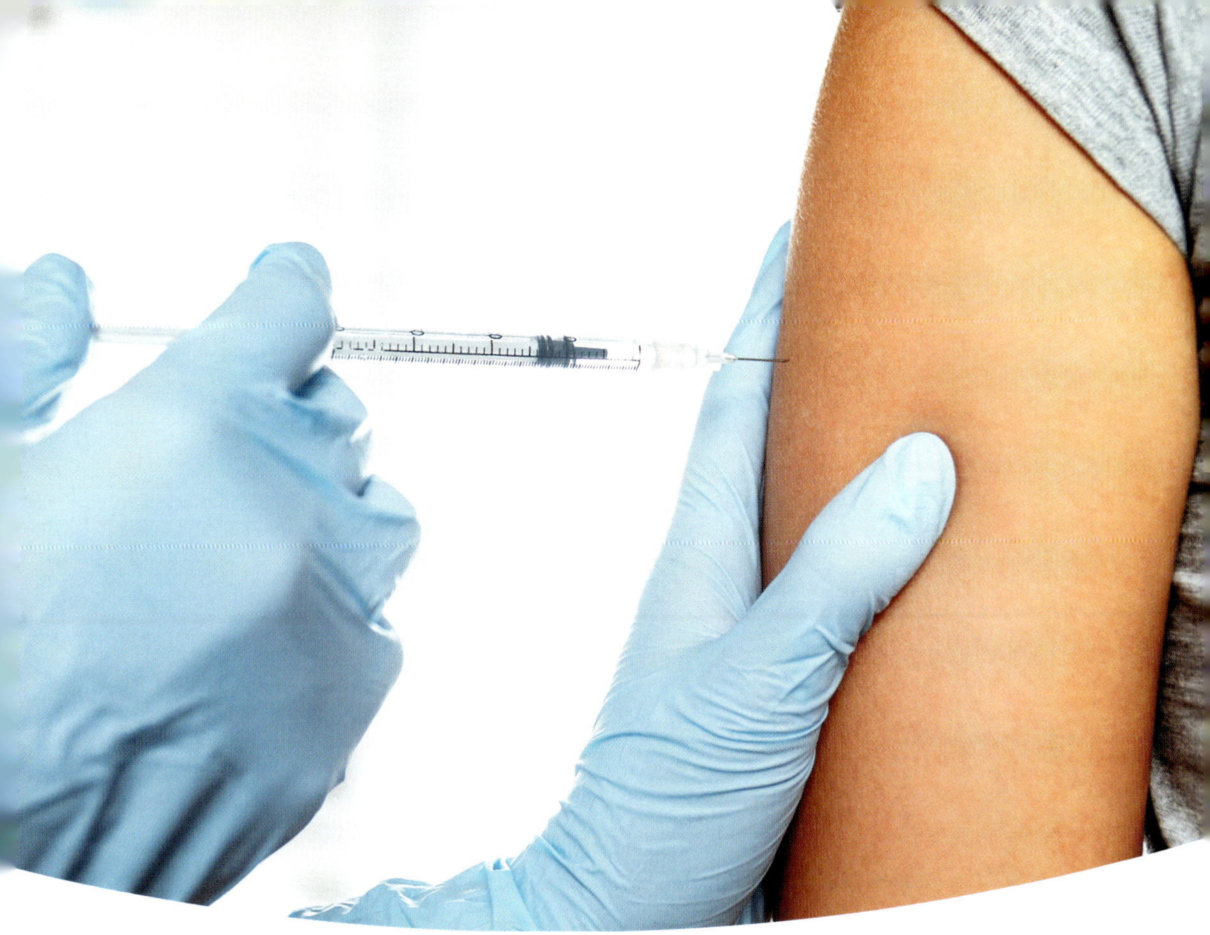

Trials test a vaccine's effectiveness.

develop in the smaller trials. They also make sure the vaccine helps the body produce antibodies. If the large trials are successful, the vaccine developer applies to the FDA for a license. The FDA inspects the factory where the vaccine will be made. It also approves the labeling of the vaccine.

Even after a vaccine is licensed, the FDA keeps a close watch on its production. FDA employees inspect facilities. They study the manufacturer's tests of the vaccine. They may even conduct their own tests on the vaccine.

Public health officials also watch for side effects. If a side effect is linked to a vaccine, they weigh the benefits of the vaccine against the possible risks. They recommend whether the vaccine should be used.

It can take 10 to 15 years to develop and test a new vaccine. But preventing a disease is almost always less expensive than treating it. In 2016, a study showed that every dollar invested in vaccines saves $16 in health care costs. If fewer people get sick, less money will be spent on hospital stays and other medical expenses. In one year, for example, hospitals in Colorado treated

Each vaccine goes though many tests to make sure that it is safe.

538 children for diseases that vaccines could have prevented. This cost $29.2 million, or more than $54,000 per child. A dose of a vaccine typically costs less than $200.

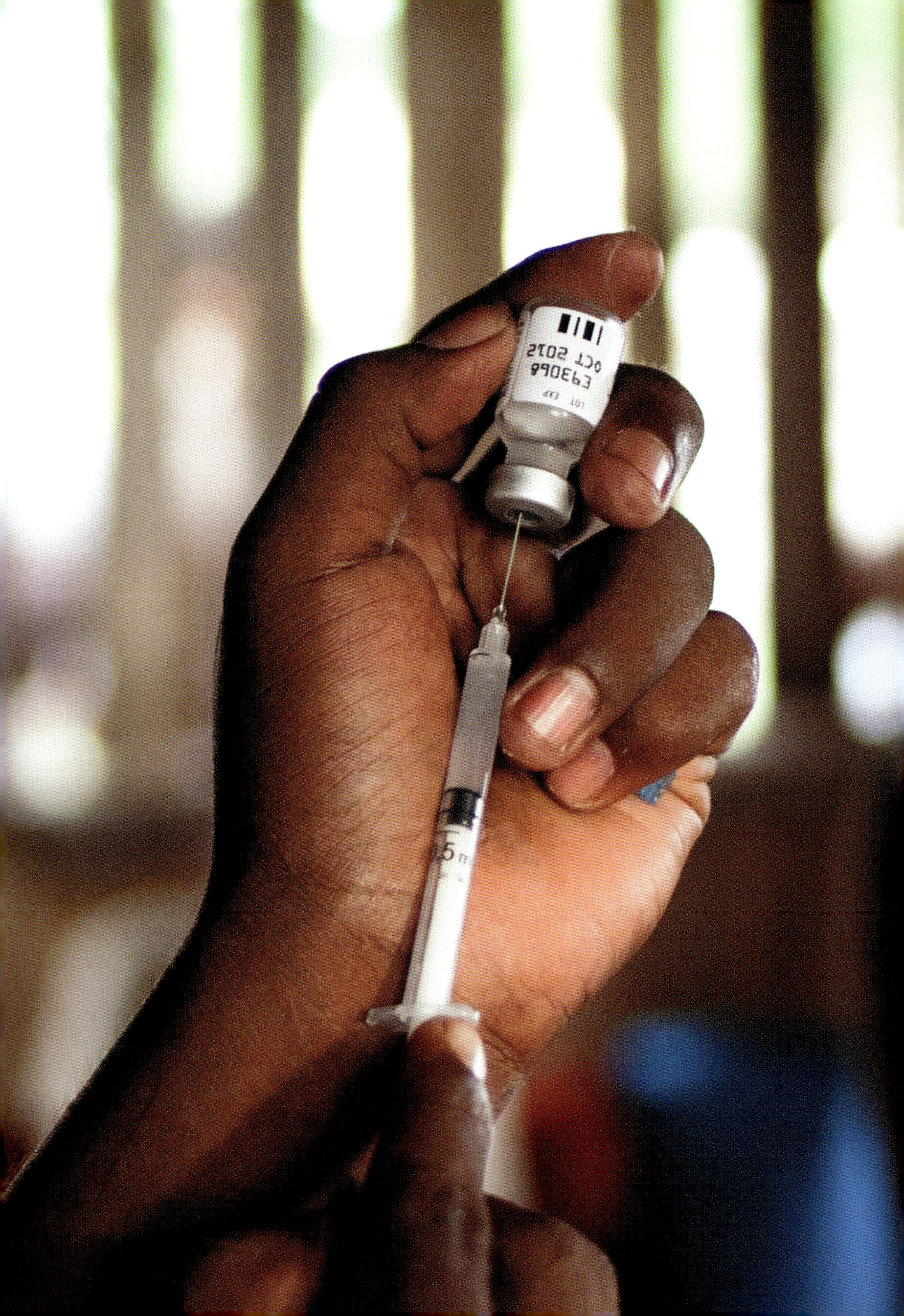

CHAPTER 4

PRO
VACCINES PROTECT THE UNVACCINATED

Not everyone can receive vaccines. For example, babies who are less than one month old are too young to get vaccines. People with serious illnesses such as cancer may not be able to receive vaccines either. But vaccines still help these people stay healthy. People who cannot receive vaccines rely on the immunity of others. If a person is immune to a disease, he or she cannot give it to someone else.

Vaccines make it more difficult for diseases to spread.

When more people are immune to a disease, it is harder for the disease to spread. This is known as herd immunity. But herd immunity breaks down when people who can receive vaccines do not. When fewer than 90 percent of children in a

HERD IMMUNITY

When people are vaccinated, they help prevent disease from spreading.

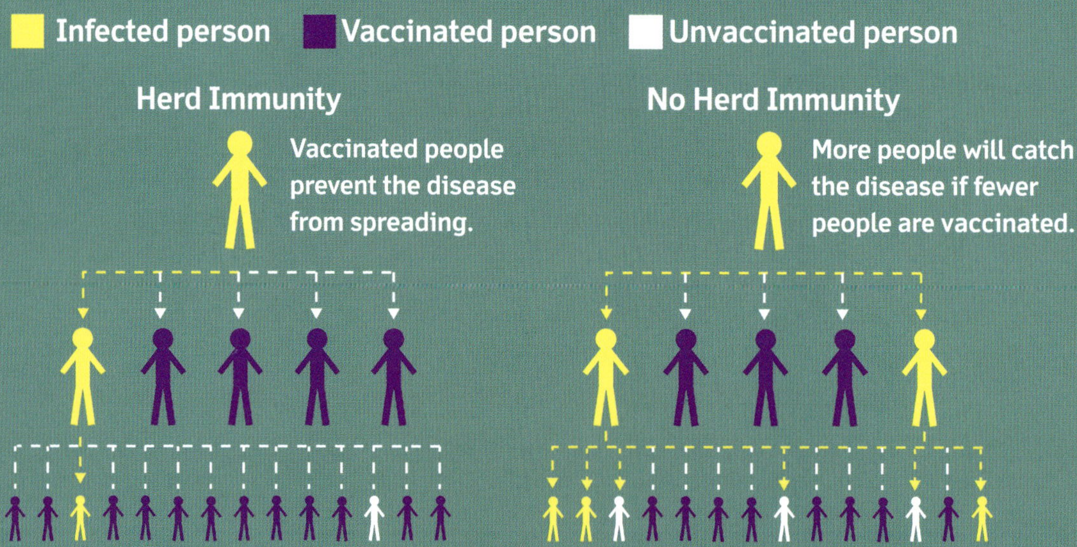

community are not vaccinated, serious diseases can spread.

Approximately 3 percent of children in the United States are not vaccinated. But these children often live in the same communities. As a result, everyone in that community is at risk. Herd immunity will no longer prevent outbreaks of disease.

Some people think that if a disease is no longer occurring, vaccinations are not necessary. However, if vaccines are stopped, it can be easier for a disease to spread. Because people travel, diseases can spread rapidly. It takes only one traveler from another country where the disease is present to spark an outbreak. Polio, measles, and other preventable diseases could be spread throughout the world.

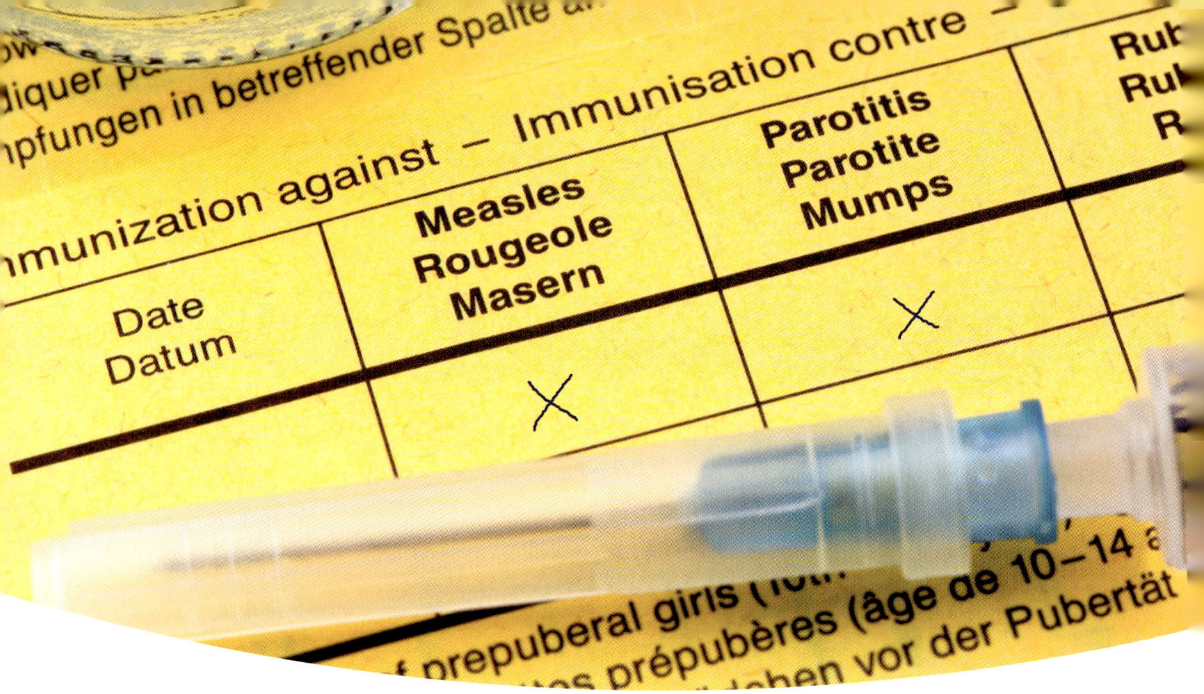

Immunization records keep track of which vaccines a person has received.

Outbreaks of serious diseases around the world have been increasing. For instance, the United States was free of measles in 2000. But some parents chose not to vaccinate their children. The herd immunity broke down. In 2011, 220 cases of measles were reported in the United States. The Centers for Disease Control linked these cases to travelers returning from countries in Europe and Southeast Asia. In 2015, an outbreak

VACCINES AND AUTISM

Autism is a disorder that makes it difficult to communicate with others. A study published in 1998 claimed that the MMR vaccine caused some children to develop autism. Later studies focused on thimerosal, a substance used in the MMR vaccine. Since 2003, however, numerous studies have shown no link between autism and the MMR vaccine. In addition, studies have shown no link between autism and thimerosal. The author of the original article even had his medical license revoked because of his dishonest study. Still, some parents choose not to vaccinate their children.

of measles occurred at a large amusement park. The virus spread quickly. It took only a small group of people who were not vaccinated to fuel the outbreak. Many children got the disease. Vaccinations could have prevented many of these cases.

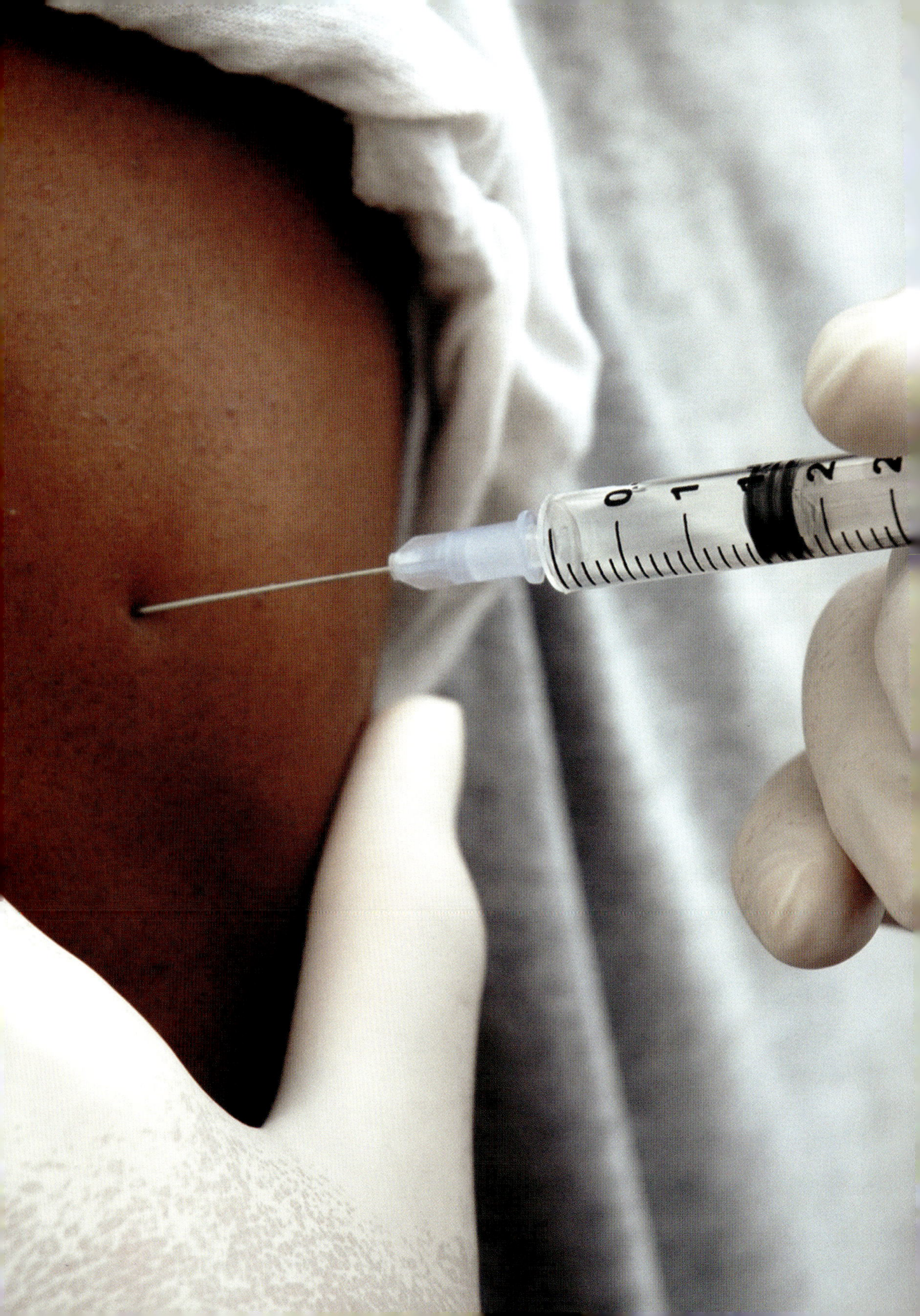

CHAPTER 5

CON
VACCINES DO NOT ALWAYS WORK

Vaccines occasionally fail to prevent a disease. Sometimes, a person's **immune system** does not respond to a vaccine. Other times, vaccines fail because people make mistakes. Vaccines, especially live ones, must be handled correctly. Most need to be kept cool. Transporting the vaccine can take a long time. Some areas may not have cold storage to keep the vaccines alive. Then the vaccines do not work.

Not all vaccines guarantee lifelong immunity.

Red Cross workers transport the measles vaccine.

Errors can also happen when the vaccine is produced. For example, flu viruses change from season to season. It is difficult for people's immune systems to recognize the new viruses. Every year, scientists must try to match the antigens in the vaccine to the flu viruses being passed around the community. The vaccine for that year must protect against hundreds of flu viruses.

Scientists must try to predict which virus will be most common. If the virus in the vaccine does not match the virus causing the infection, people will not be immune. Even when there is a good match, the vaccine only reduces the risk of flu by approximately 50 to 60 percent.

THE MUTATING FLU

Some flu viruses can live in animals. These viruses **mutate**. In some cases, they can cause sickness in humans. Scientists are constantly studying flu viruses. They pay close attention to viruses that begin where people and animals live close together. But staying one step ahead of the flu virus is very difficult.

Depending on how long the flu season lasts, a different flu virus can begin to circulate and make people sick. Developing a vaccine for this new virus can take months. It is also very expensive.

Other vaccines require multiple doses. Vaccines may be less effective when people do not complete the full number of doses. For example, the mumps vaccine requires several doses. If children receive one dose, they may be only 78 percent immune to the disease. Two doses of the vaccine will be approximately 88 percent effective. In some cases, even the full amount of doses may not completely protect a person from the disease.

Some vaccines cannot provide permanent immunity. People must receive booster doses. These additional doses expose the body to the antigens again. People must keep getting more

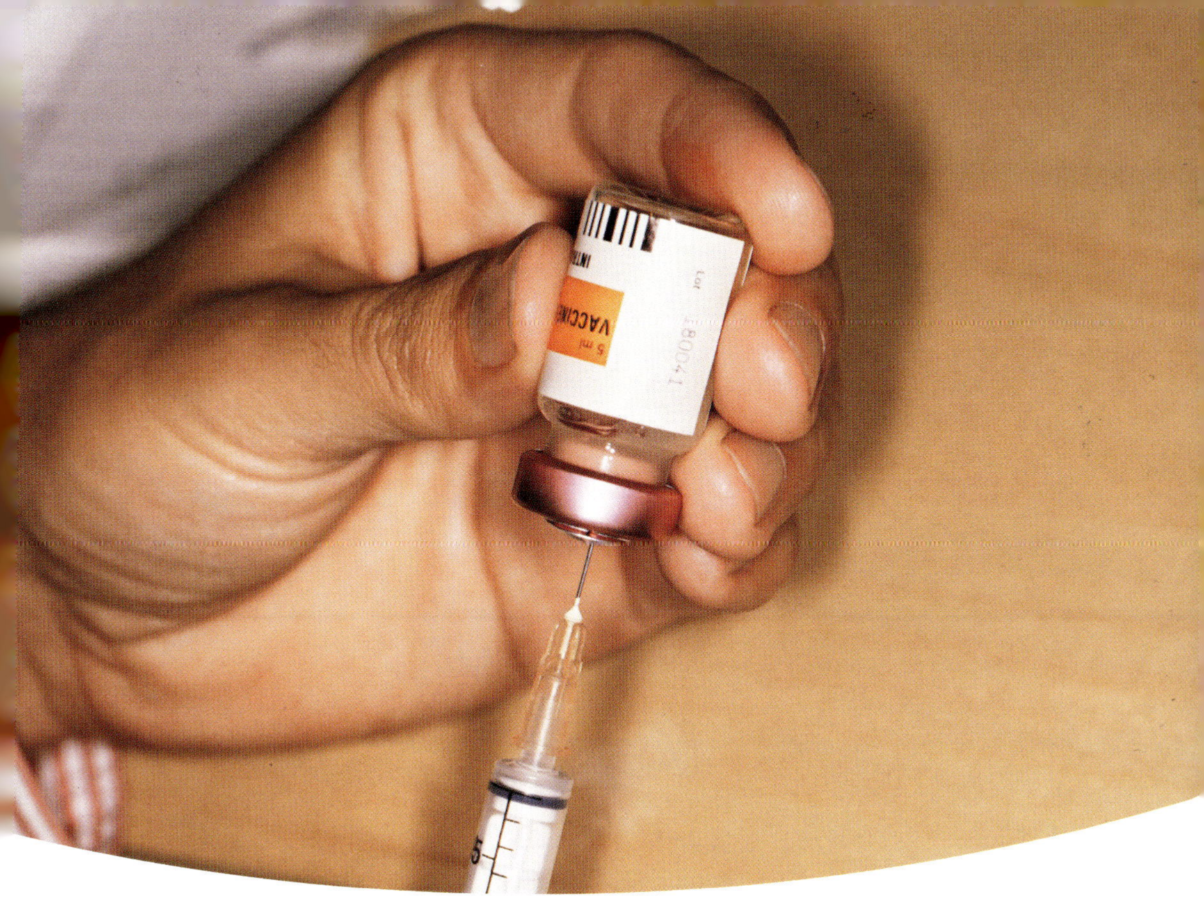

Most people who get tetanus today have not had a booster shoot.

doses to stay immune. The tetanus vaccine, for example, lasts for approximately 10 years. After that, people must get a booster dose of the vaccine to stay immune. Other vaccines have shorter periods. For example, a typhoid vaccine must be given every two to five years.

CHAPTER 6

CON
NOT EVERYONE SHOULD BE VACCINATED

A few vaccines contain ingredients that certain people are allergic to. For example, the yellow fever vaccine uses a virus that is grown in eggs. This vaccine contains a small amount of egg protein. People who are allergic to eggs could have a reaction to the vaccine. To avoid a reaction, they must go through a desensitization process. They must get several shots instead of only one. Each shot contains a small dose of the vaccine.

People in South America, Central America, and Africa may be at risk of catching yellow fever.

An allergist gives the shots one at a time. The amount of vaccine in each shot is increased.

Gelatin can also cause people to have allergic reactions. The vaccines for chicken pox, yellow fever, and the flu use gelatin. Gelatin is the most common cause of an allergic reaction to a vaccine. However, reactions to gelatin are still rare.

People with damaged or weak immune systems are at risk, too. Vaccines might not work for them. These people's immune systems do not work properly. Cancer patients receiving radiation or medication often have damaged immune systems. So do people with human immunodeficiency virus (HIV), heart disease, and other chronic illnesses.

Organ transplant patients are given large doses of medicine to reduce their immunity. This helps prevent their bodies from rejecting the new

The vaccine for measles, mumps, and rubella (MMR) contains gelatin.

organs. However, it also weakens their immune systems.

People with weak immune systems are often warned not to receive vaccinations. Often, their bodies will not produce immunity to the disease.

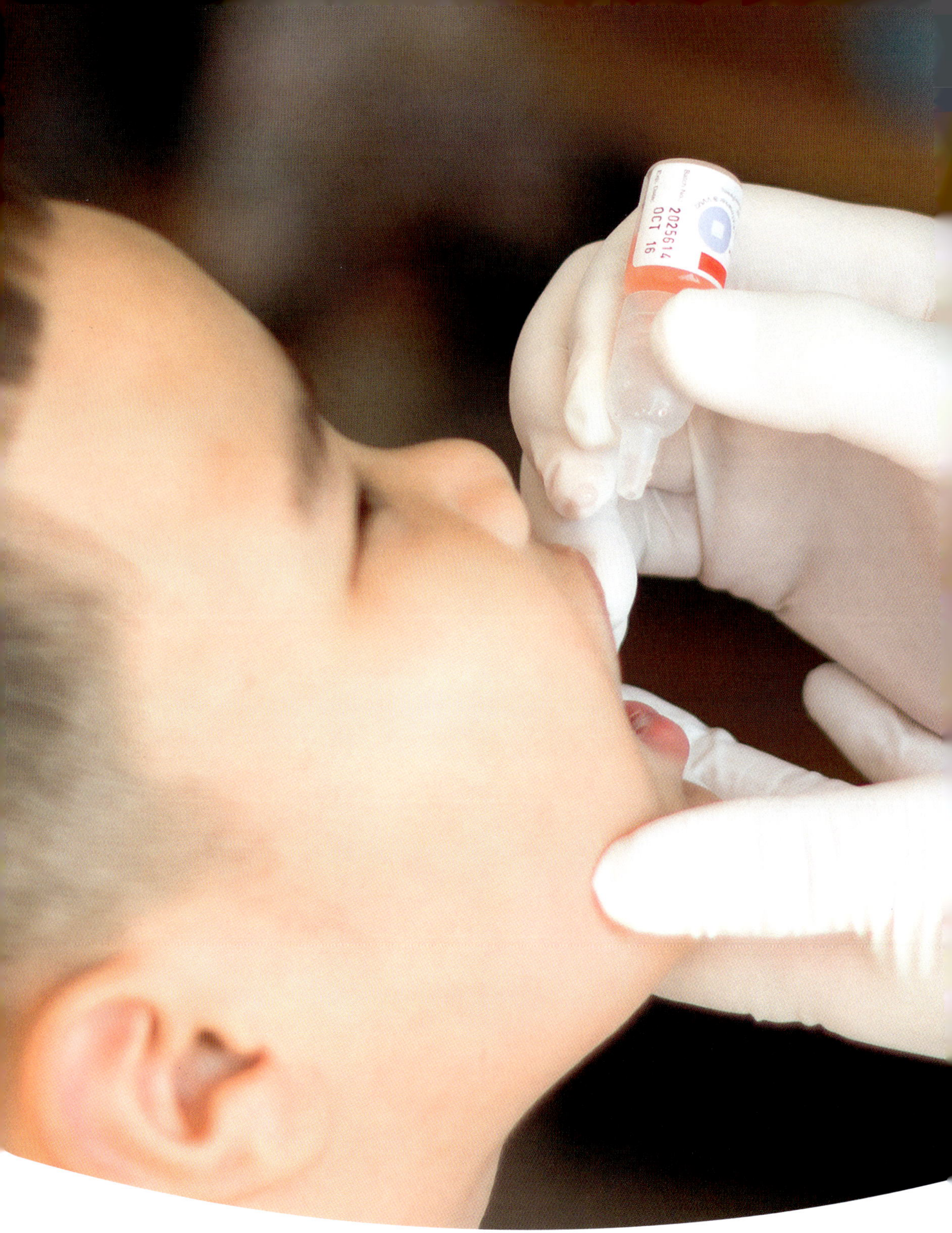

The oral polio vaccine only prevents approximately 50 percent of people from getting the disease.

DID YOU KNOW?

Approximately one in one million children has a life-threatening allergic reaction to vaccines. Signs of a severe allergic reaction include hives and difficulty breathing.

In some cases, the vaccine may even harm them. Their bodies may not be able to fight the viruses in some vaccines.

Live vaccines pose the biggest threat to people with weak immune systems. Measles, polio, and chicken pox vaccines usually contain live viruses. Live viruses are used to make nasal mist flu vaccines. People with weak immune systems cannot fight off the live germs in these vaccines. They may develop an infection. The vaccines may make them sick.

CHAPTER 7

CON
VACCINES CAN CAUSE SIDE EFFECTS

Some vaccines have side effects. These side effects are not nearly as serious as the diseases that the vaccines prevent. But they are still unpleasant. For example, vaccines for chicken pox and measles can cause a mild fever or rash. But these reactions usually do not last long.

Although it is rare, vaccines can have more serious side effects. A few people have had difficulty breathing after receiving vaccines.

Some children develop redness and swelling where the shot was given.

Others had rapid heartbeats or chest pain. Some felt dizzy or faint. People have also reported nausea, vomiting, or diarrhea after receiving a vaccine.

In a few cases, side effects are severe. For example, the MMR vaccine causes **seizures** in approximately one in 3,000 doses. In extremely rare cases, some people have suffered deafness or permanent brain damage after the MMR vaccine.

According to some sources, the chicken pox vaccine may cause seizures or other severe reactions. A few children have developed pneumonia after getting this vaccine.

DID YOU KNOW?

Approximately one-fourth of people feel temporary pain in their joints after the MMR vaccine.

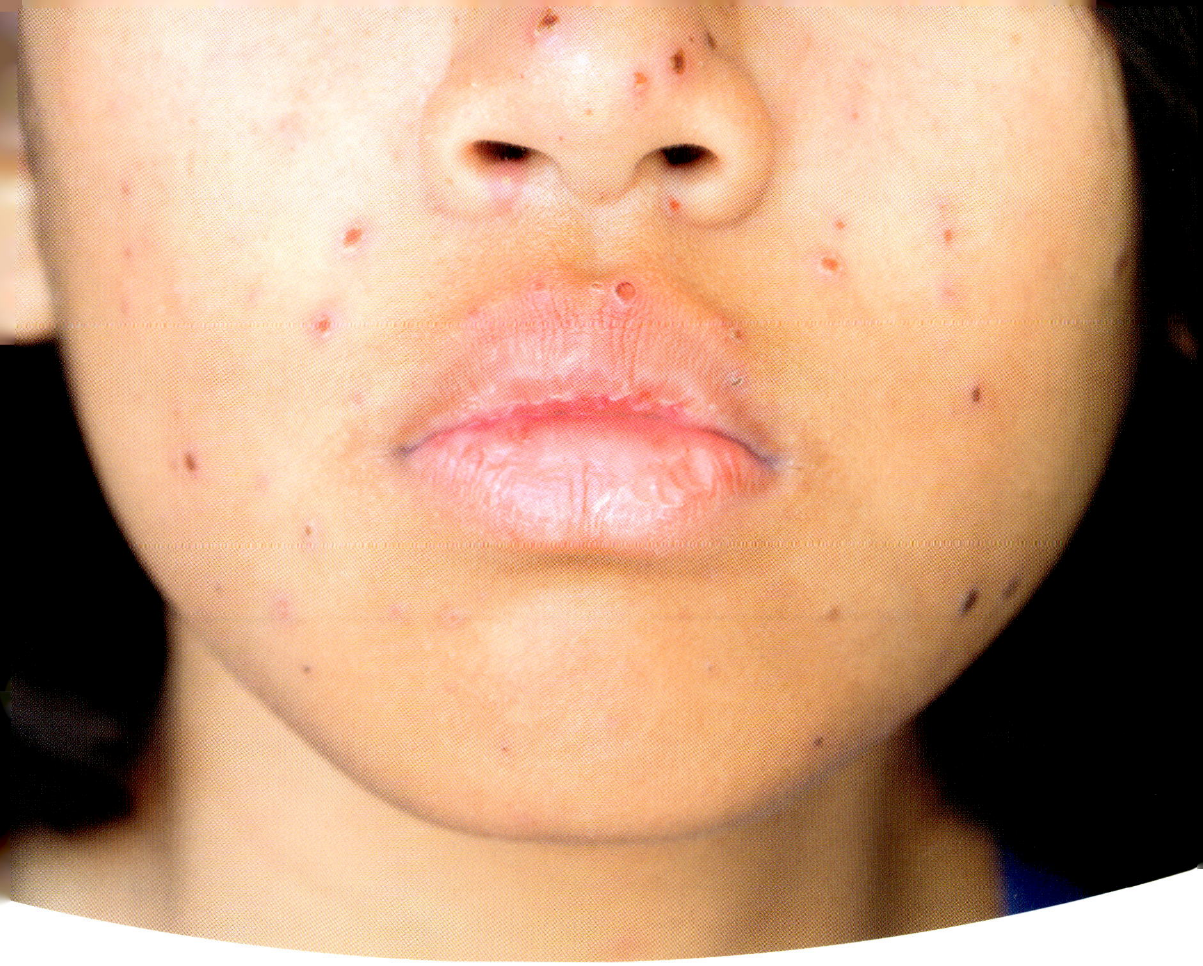

The chicken pox virus causes a rash of painful blisters.

Plus, the chicken pox vaccine uses a live virus. Family members can be exposed to the disease when a child is vaccinated. Adults and teenagers may develop serious complications if they get chicken pox.

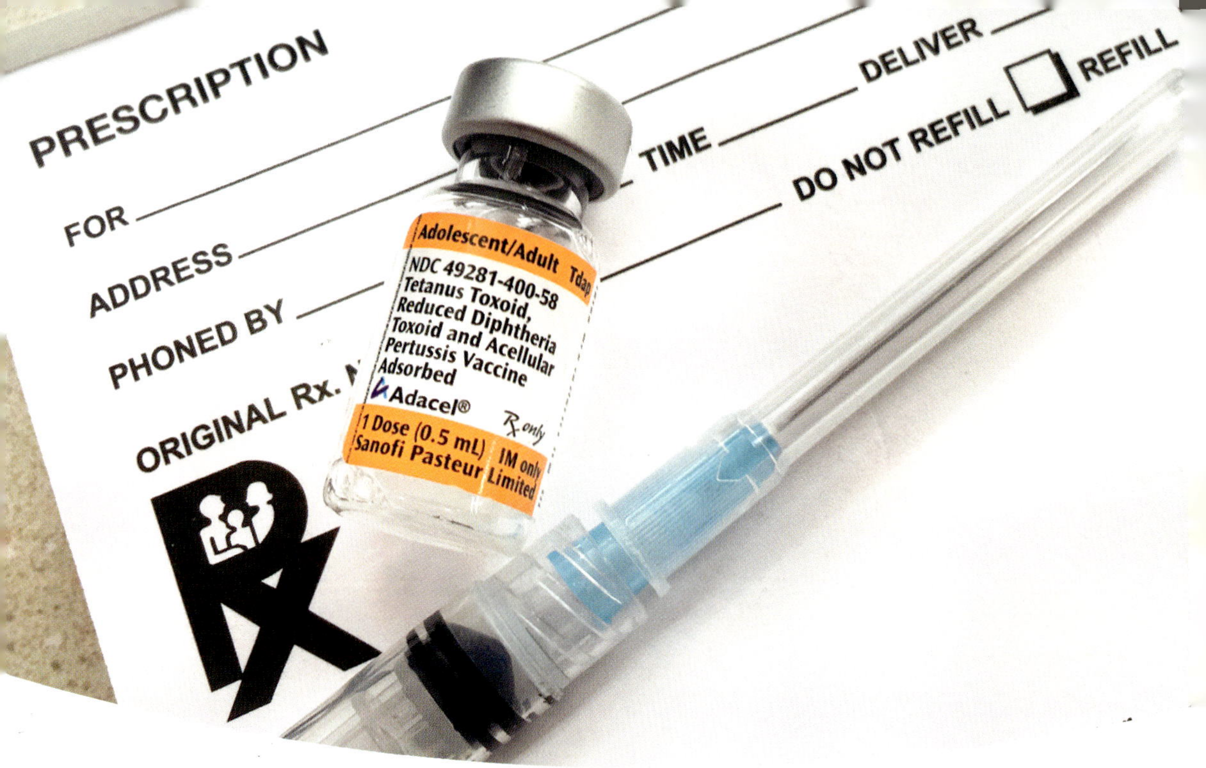

In 2010, approximately 75 people died after receiving the tetanus vaccine.

In 1990, the United States created the Vaccine **Adverse** Event Reporting System. Since then, approximately 30,000 cases of harmful reactions to vaccines have been reported each year. Approximately 85 to 90 percent of these reactions are mild. But 10 to 15 percent are serious. This means the vaccines have caused permanent disability, life-threatening illness, or death.

A few people have died after receiving a vaccine, though this is very uncommon. In 1994, approximately 160 people died after getting a tetanus shot. That same year, approximately 140 people died after getting a polio vaccine. But this number varies from year to year. Other years, fewer than 100 people died after getting the vaccine for tetanus or polio.

The flu and pneumonia vaccines have the most risk of causing death. More than 100 people in the United States die each year after receiving these vaccines. But that is still a very small percentage of the millions of people who get these vaccines.

It is important to weigh the benefits of vaccines against the possible side effects. Some people are at greater risk for side effects than others. Before getting a vaccine, each person should talk with his or her doctor.

PROS

- Vaccines protect people from dangerous diseases and complications.
- Vaccines have reduced the number of deaths caused by illnesses.
- The FDA's system of testing and trials ensures that vaccines are developed and manufactured safely.
- Vaccinating against a disease is less expensive than treating it.
- Vaccines have greatly reduced outbreaks of serious diseases worldwide.
- Herd immunity even protects people who cannot get vaccines.

CONS

- Errors in vaccine production or storage can lead to vaccines that do not work.
- People must receive multiple doses of some vaccines to produce immunity.
- A few people are allergic to ingredients that are used to make vaccines.
- Some people are not able to receive vaccines.
- Vaccines can have unpleasant side effects.
- In extremely rare cases, side effects from vaccines can be serious or even life-threatening.

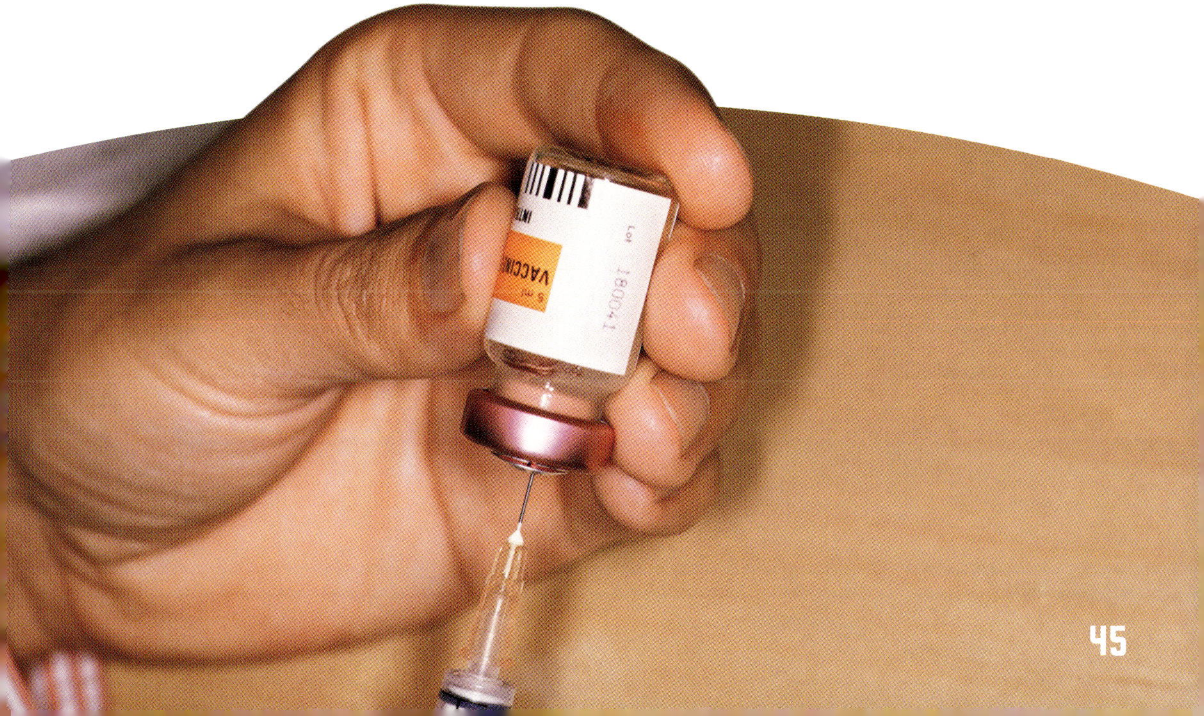

FOCUS ON

VACCINES

Write your answers on a separate piece of paper.

1. Write a paragraph explaining how vaccines create immunity.
2. If you were a parent, would you vaccinate your child? Why or why not?
3. Which vaccine requires a booster shot every 10 years?
   - A. mumps
   - B. polio
   - C. tetanus
4. Why are vaccines tested on a larger group during the third phrase?
   - A. Using larger groups can reveal side effects that are too rare to happen in the smaller trials.
   - B. Using larger groups can increase the likelihood that the vaccine will produce immunity.
   - C. Using larger groups can help spread the news about the new vaccine.

Answer key on page 48.

GLOSSARY

adverse
Creating harmful results.

antibodies
Proteins that fight infections by attaching themselves to antigens and destroying them.

antigens
Proteins that disease-causing organisms use to attach themselves to cells in the infected body.

complications
Medical problems that arise in addition to the main disease being treated.

immune system
The body system that uses specialized cells to fight infections.

membranes
Thin layers of tissue that cover some parts inside the body.

mutate
To develop a new trait as a result of changes to genes.

nervous system
The body system that picks up and sends nerve impulses to other parts of the body.

paralyzed
Unable to move a part of the body.

pneumonia
The infection of one or both lungs.

seizures
Extreme twitching of muscles because of unusual brain activity.

TO LEARN MORE

BOOKS

Hand, Carol. *Vaccines*. Minneapolis: Abdo Publishing, 2014.

Rissman, Rebecca. *The Vaccination Debate*. Minneapolis: Abdo Publishing, 2016.

Yomtov, Nel. *From African Plant to Vaccine Preservative*. Ann Arbor, MI: Cherry Lake, 2014.

NOTE TO EDUCATORS

Visit **www.focusreaders.com** to find lesson plans, activities, links, and other resources related to this title.

INDEX

Answer Key: 1. Answers will vary; **2.** Answers will vary; **3.** C; **4.** A